BUTTERSCOTCH

(THE FLAVOR OF THE INVISIBLE)

BUTTERSCOTCH
(The Flavor of the Invisible)

Written and illustrated by
Milo Manara

Translated from the French
"Le Parfum de l'Invisible"
by Tom Leighton
Edited by Bernd Metz

Published by Catalan Communications
43 E. 19th Street
New York, NY 10003

© 1987 by Milo Manara. Agent: L. Staletti, Paris
English language edition © 1987 by Catalan Communications

ISBN 0-87416-047-2
Dep. L. B. 40.392-87

First Printing October 1987
Printed in Catalonia (Spain)

MILO MANARA

BUTTERSCOTCH

(THE FLAVOR OF THE INVISIBLE)

catalan communications
new york

I'M A PHYSICS PROFESSOR... WHILE CONDUCTING MY RESEARCH... YOU UNDERSTAND... I JUST HAPPENED QUITE BY CHANCE TO DISCOVER THAT OPTICAL FIBERS... I MEAN WASTE OPTICAL FIBERS... TO MAKE A LONG STORY SHORT... I MADE A KIND OF OINTMENT WHICH DOESN'T REFLECT LIGHT IN THE NORMAL WAY...

LET'S JUST SAY THAT ANY OBJECT COVERED WITH THIS OINTMENT BECOMES INVISIBLE. YOU JUST CAN'T SEE IT ANYMORE!

OF COURSE, IN ADDITION TO OPTICAL FIBERS, I HAD TO USE A BASE... A NON-TOXIC BASE... THE IDEAL SUBSTANCE WAS BUTTER-SCOTCH... DO YOU FOLLOW ME... THAT'S WHY THIS OINTMENT HAS THIS FLAVOR...

COME NOW, THE SMELL ISN'T REALLY SO AWFUL, IS IT?

WHAT... WHAT ARE YOU DOING IN BEATRICE'S ROOM?

EVER SINCE BEATRICE BECAME A PRIMA BALLERINA, I HAVEN'T BEEN ABLE TO GET NEAR HER...

THIS IS A LIVING NIGHTMARE, AND I'M RIGHT IN THE MIDDLE OF IT!

DON'T YOU SEE, I... I'M GOING TO MAKE MY DISCOVERY PUBLIC, BUT JUST NOT RIGHT AWAY... I WANT TO SPEND A FEW DAYS BY BEATRICE'S SIDE FIRST. THAT'S WHY I'M IN HER ROOM, HERE, AT THE GRAND HOTEL... I LOVE BEATRICE... I'VE ALWAYS LOVED HER... AND JUST MAYBE SHE LOVES ME TOO...

16

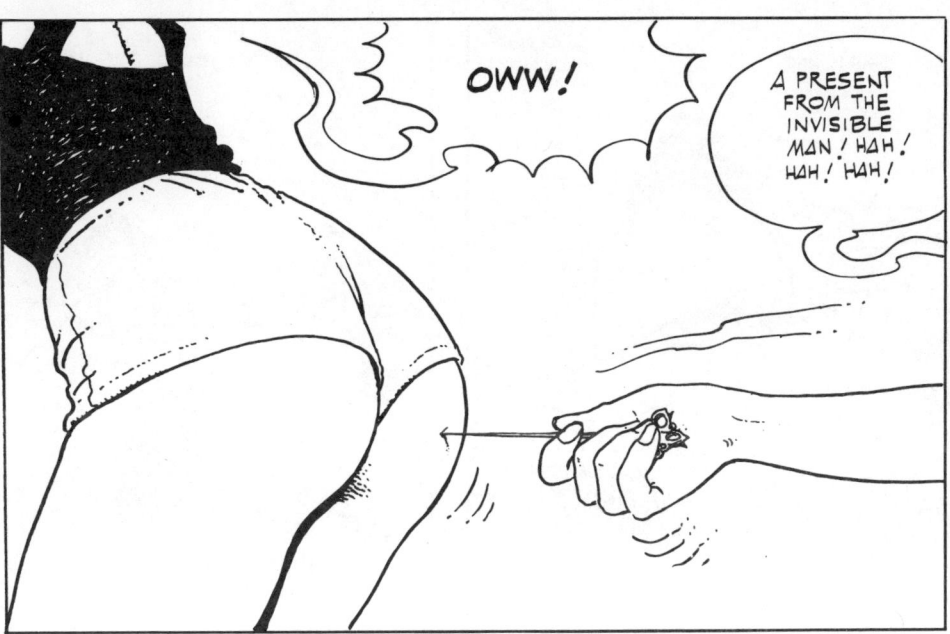

OH YEAH? SO THAT MEANS YOU DIDN'T HEAR WHAT BEATRICE SAID TO ME, RIGHT?

NO, NOTHING, NOTHING AT ALL, MISS.

WELL, YOU JUST MISSED SEEING YOUR BELOVED WITH HER PANTIES DOWN, A REAL SHOW!

PLEASE! I'D NEVER DREAM OF... YOU MISJUDGE ME... MISS... YOU WERE THE FIRST ONE WHO HAD EVER TOUCHED ME... HAS TOUCHED ME... I NEVER HAD ANY CONTACT WITH A WOMAN BEFORE YOU, MISS...

LOOK, YOU KNOW... I ONLY TOUCHED YOU BECAUSE YOU'RE A DREAM. I DON'T JUST GO RUNNING AROUND FEELING UP THE PRICK OF EVERY GUY AROUND, YOU KNOW!

NO, NO, THAT'S NOT WHAT I...

YOU'RE A REAL HOOT, BUTTERSCOTCH! I CAN ALMOST SEE YOU BLUSHING!

HEY THERE! YOU'RE STILL STIFF! DOESN'T IT START TO HURT?

NO... PLEASE... DON'T TOUCH THERE... I...

DON'T YOU WANT ME TO HELP YOU UNLOAD YOUR RIFLE?...

NO, DON'T DO THAT... OOOHHH... DON'T...OOHH...

JUST A LITTLE BIT MORE AND IT'LL BE ALL BETTER... THE GUARD CAN GO OFF DUTY...

THERE SHE IS! IT'S BEATRICE D'ALTAVILLA!

DAMN! THAT PARTY-POOPER'S HERE TO SPOIL EVERYTHING!

OOOHHH... OOOHHH...

19

I UNDERSTOOD RIGHT AWAY YOU WERE A POOR WIMP!

ANY REAL MAN, WHO FOUND OUT HOW TO BE INVISIBLE, WOULD HAVE GONE OUT AND ROBBED A BANK, LAYED ALL THE MOST GORGEOUS CHICKS...

OR, I DON'T KNOW... KNOCKED OFF A GUY LIKE QADDAFI OR THE POPE, OR SOMETHING...

ONLY A MORON LIKE YOU WOULD JUST BE HAPPY SNIFFING AFTER A NO-TALENT DANCER WHO HAS A CAREER THANKS TO...

STOP IT! IF YOU GO ON INSULTING BEATRICE, WHY I'LL...

YOU'LL WHAT? WHAT'LL YOU DO TO ME THIS TIME, HUH? HIT ME AGAIN?

PLEASE! DON'T TALK LIKE THAT! A WHILE AGO I... I LOST MY HEAD! I JUST... I LOVE BEATRICE!

OK, OK! SO YOU CAN DROP DEAD FROM LOVING THAT SLUT IF YOU WANT TO, THAT DOESN'T GIVE YOU THE RIGHT TO HIT SOMEBODY!

QUIET!... QUIET!

LISTEN GOOD, FELLAH. YOU'RE JUST LIKE ALL THE OTHER ASSHOLES. YOU THINK SHE'S SOME ANGEL WHEN ALL THE TIME SHE'S WORSE THAN THE DEVIL HIMSELF, SHE'S A...

A SADISTIC BITCH AND... OOOHH!

THAT'S IT, GO ON, HIT ME! THAT DOESN'T STOP HER BEING A SLUT! A DIRTY SLUT!

SNIFF... SNIFF...

HEY, YOU! I THOUGHT I MADE MYSELF CLEAR! I DON'T WANT TO SMELL YOU AROUND ANYMORE!

ERR... I DON'T KNOW WHAT TO SAY TO MAKE YOU FORGIVE ME, MISS... I WAS TERRIBLE, I KNOW... I'M SO ASHAMED OF WHAT I DID... YOU DON'T KNOW HOW SORRY...

BEAT IT, GODDAMN IT, OR YOU'LL REALLY BE SORRY!

THIS IS MY SECRETARY! OF COURSE, THE IDIOT DIDN'T HAVE ENOUGH SENSE TO DRESS DECENTLY!

COME, COME, DON'T BE HARD ON HER, THIS SPONTANEITY OF HERS IS TOTALLY CHARMING!

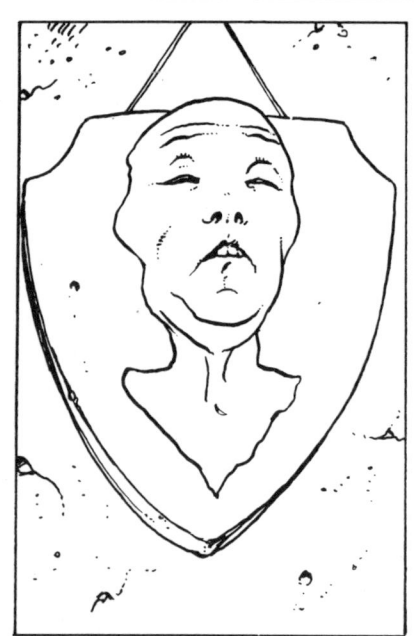

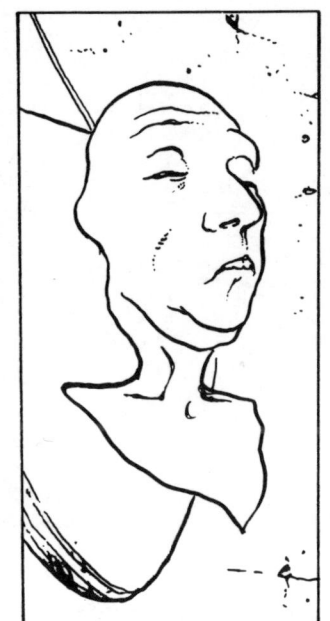

SO! YOU'RE NOT FLINCHING? GREAT, OK! I KNOW JUST HOW TO GET YOU TO REACT...

HA, HA! YOU FEEL THAT, DON'T YOU, HUH? YOU JUST LOVE IT!

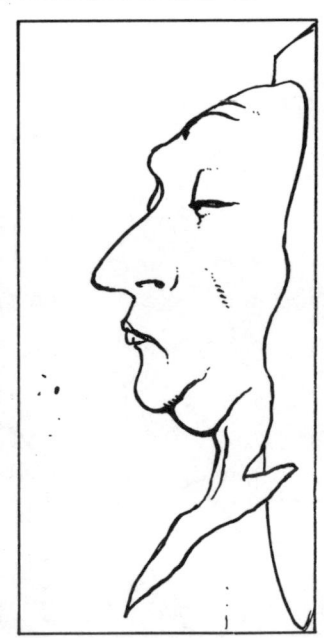

STOP PRETENDING YOU DON'T FEEL ANYTHING, PAL! I CAN FEEL YOU SEE WHAT I'M GETTING AT... MORE AND MORE.

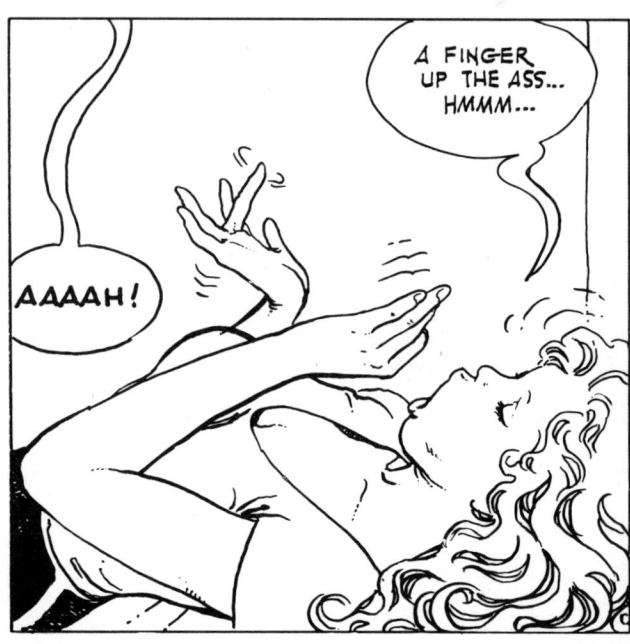

YOU HEAR ME? I KNOW YOU'RE HERE, I CAN SMELL YOU!

SO, HERE YOU ARE!

30

HIDING UNDER A SHEET! I'D HAVE GIVEN YOU MORE CREDIT THAN THAT, PAL!

HEY... WHO... WHO...

MISS! GO BACK DOWNSTAIRS RIGHT NOW! WHO GAVE YOU PERMISSION TO...

DID YOU HEAR? COME DOWN RIGHT NOW! MY WORD, YOU NEED HELP!

YOU UNDERSTAND NOW? STOP NOW, NO ONE WILL BELIEVE YOUR STORY, THEY'LL LOCK YOU UP!

OH, I KNEW YOU WERE HERE, YOU SHITHEAD!

31

33

35

WHY DO THEY CALL YOU HONEY?

OK, WELL, IT'S BECAUSE I TASTE REAL SWEET, THAT'S WHAT THEY SAY!

YOU TASTE REAL... REAL SS... SWEET?

THAT'S WHAT THEY SAY... YOU DON'T BELIEVE ME, HUH? WHAT DON'T YOU BELIEVE? THAT THEY SAY IT OR THAT I TASTE REAL SWEET?

I--- I...

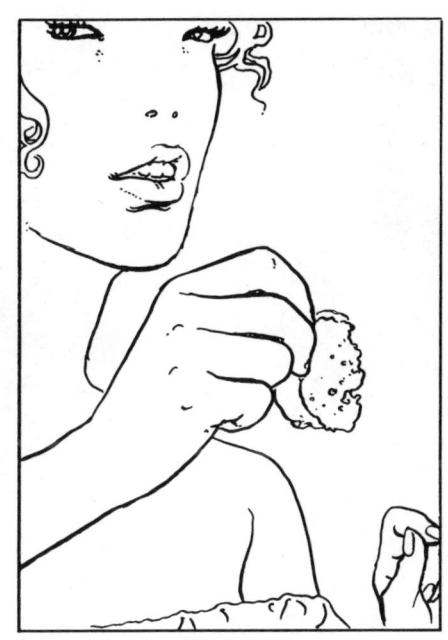

HERE, GO ON... HAVE A TASTE!

IT'S... IT'S TRUE... SHE IS... VERY SWEET!

YOU SEE ?! I'D DON'T NEED TO PUT ON ANY BUTTERSCOTCH!

HONEY!

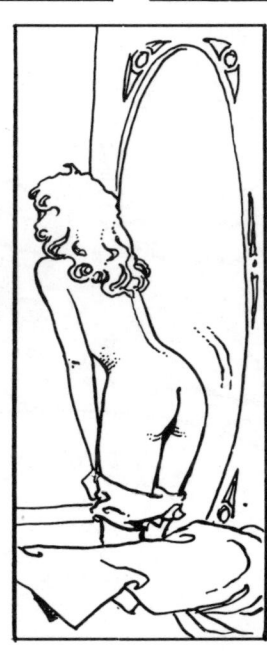

FOR YOU IT MUST BE VERY HARD TO BELIEVE IN THE PURITY OF MY LOVE FOR BEATRICE...

YEP! EVER SINCE I'VE KNOW YOU, YOU HAVEN'T GONE ONE SECOND WITHOUT A HARD-ON.

WAIT, WAIT...!

TAKE A LOOK AT THIS PICTURE.

SEE? IT'S BEATRICE AND ME WHEN WE WERE TEN YEARS OLD. ALREADY I WAS MADLY IN LOVE WITH HER.

SEE WHAT SHE'S HOLDING IN HER ARMS? IT'S A LITTLE WOLF. I DREW IT AND CUT IT OUT OF CARDBOARD MYSELF.

YOU KNOW THE WOLF IS A SYMBOL OF FREEDOM... AND ON THE BACK... ON THE BACK OF THE WOLF I WROTE...

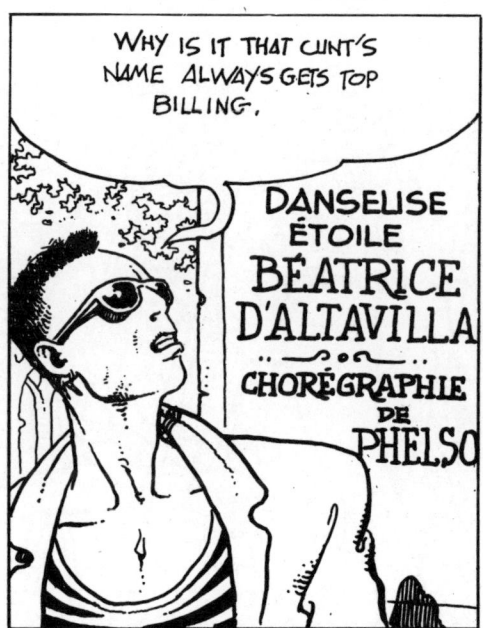

44

I DON'T KNOW WHAT IT MEANT... I USED IT TO START A FIRE ONCE...

AT THAT AGE WE USED TO LIGHT FIRES ALL THE TIME. BUT WHAT WE LIKED BEST WAS PUTTING THEM OUT, HA HA!

SNIFF!

SHIT, WHO'S THAT SNIFFLING?

HEY, WHAT'S THAT FUCKING WET STUFF?

IT'S RAINING! QUICK, LET'S RUN BACK TO THE HOTEL!

...BUT BEATRICE, THE SUN'S OUT!

IF I SAY IT'S RAINING, IT'S RAINING! BACK IN THE HOTEL RIGHT NOW!

45

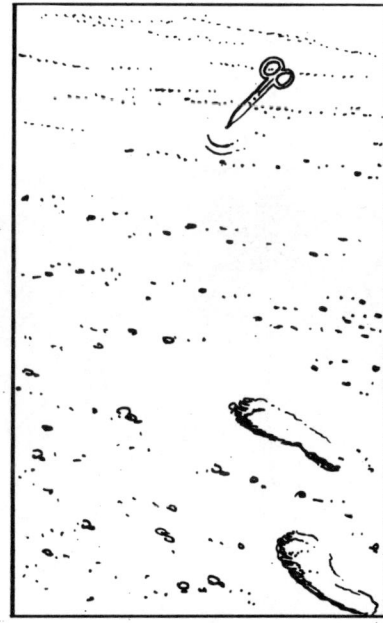

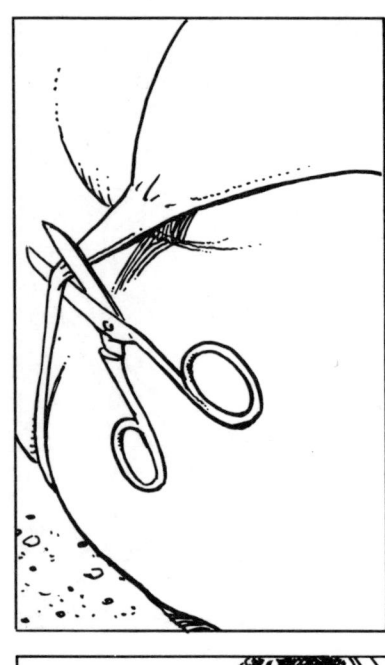

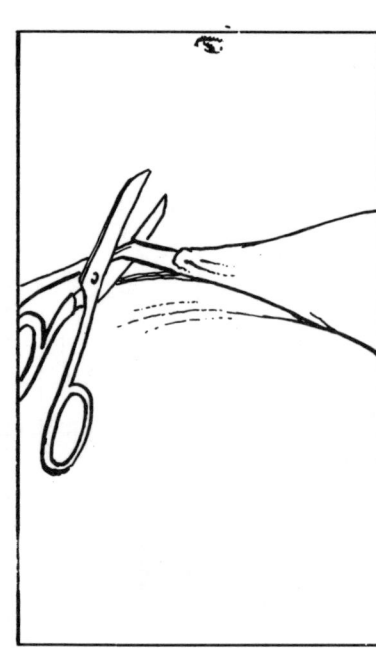

CLARA.!! WHAT... ARE YOU CRAZY?!

...HUH? WHAT? OOOOH.!!

BITCH, COVER YOURSELF UP. HEY, WHAT ARE YOU ALL STARING AT, HUH?!

HEY?!...WHAT THE...?!

NO, NO, LEAVE ME ALONE!

SHE'S CRAZY, NO ONE'S EVEN NEAR HER.

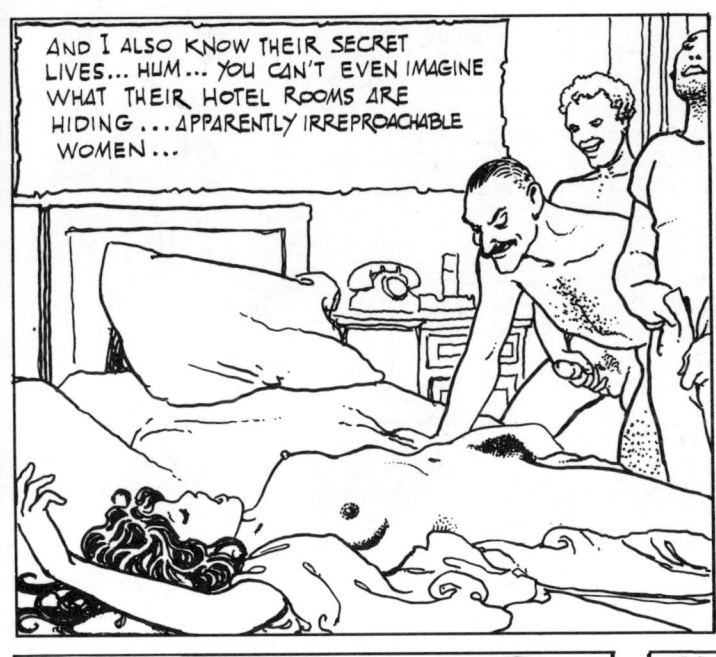

AND I ALSO KNOW THEIR SECRET LIVES... HUM... YOU CAN'T EVEN IMAGINE WHAT THEIR HOTEL ROOMS ARE HIDING... APPARENTLY IRREPROACHABLE WOMEN...

OR WHAT YOU MIGHT DISCOVER INSIDE TENTS ON CAMPING GROUNDS... THERE ARE TIMES I JUST CAN'T... RESIST...

... AND I CREATE EMBARRASSING, SCANDALOUS SITUATIONS... JUST TO SEE THEIR PRETTY EYES WIDE OPEN...

SOMETIMES I WENT TOO FAR... BUT... BUT I NEVER MANAGED TO OVERCOME MY INSATIABLE DESIRE...

... JUST BY TAKING HOLD OF AN UNSUSPECTING FEMALE HAND AND GUIDING IT... I CAN START THINGS THAT...

... GIVE BIRTH TO EROIC FURY... AND I IMAGINE... YES... I IMAGINE THE PUSSY GETTING WET...

... GO ON... LICK IT... LICK IT...

... A PUSSY MAKES ME DIZZY WITH LUST... ENDLESSLY... AND I'D DO ANYTHING AT ALL TO SATISFY HER... EVEN THE MOST INTIMATE... THE MOST IMPOSSIBLY DELICIOUS...

... SOMETIMES... WHIPPED CREAM ISN'T EXACTLY WHAT I SPURT INTO THOSE SURPRISED, INNOCENT MOUTHS...

... YES... I HAPPEN SOMETIMES TO LOSE ALL CONTROL JUST AT THE THOUGHT THAT EVERY WOMAN HAS A PUSSY UNDER HER SKIRT!...

... AND I WANT TO SHOW IT OFF TO THE WORLD...

...PUSSY... PUSSY... PUSSY... I DON'T BELIEVE IN ANYTHING ELSE IN THE WORLD OR ALMOST... HMM... ONLY THE PUSSY EXISTS, IT GIVES MEANING TO OUR LIVES... IT ASSURES US OF IMMORTALITY...

WHEN I SCAN THE SKIES WITH THE MINOTAUR'S TELESCOPE, I DON'T SEE STARS, I DON'T SEE PLANETS OR THEIR SATELLITES... HMM... I SEE A BIG, AN IMMENSE... PUSSY... A SHUDDERING PUSSY... BEGINNING AND END OF EVERYTHING... EVERYTHING.

OHHH.!... YOU MAKE ME DIE... NOW THAT YOU KNOW... THAT YOU'VE UNDERSTOOD, I CAN TELL YOU WHAT BEATRICE REALLY IS...

... SHE ISN'T MY BEATRICE ANY MORE...

RIGHT BEFORE THE START OF A SHOW... WHEN THE CURTAIN IS STILL DOWN... YOUR BEAUTIFUL BALLERINA PUTS A LITTLE SATIN MASK OVER HER EYES AND THEN...

... SHE CALLS FOR BOB AND HAS HIM EXCITE HER RIGHT TO THE EDGE OF ORGASM... RIGHT THERE, ON THE STAGE... RIGHT IN FRONT OF THE TECHNICIANS AND HER PARTNERS...

... IF ONLY PEOPLE KNEW THAT... HER CAREER WOULD BE FINISHED...

THAT'S THE CHASTE BEATRICE!... EVER SINGLE TIME BEFORE GOING OUT ON STAGE... SHE HAS HERSELF LICKED UNTIL SHE GLOWS IN THE DARK... JUST LIKE YOU'RE DOING TO ME RIGHT NOW.

HM HM HM... HM HM HM...

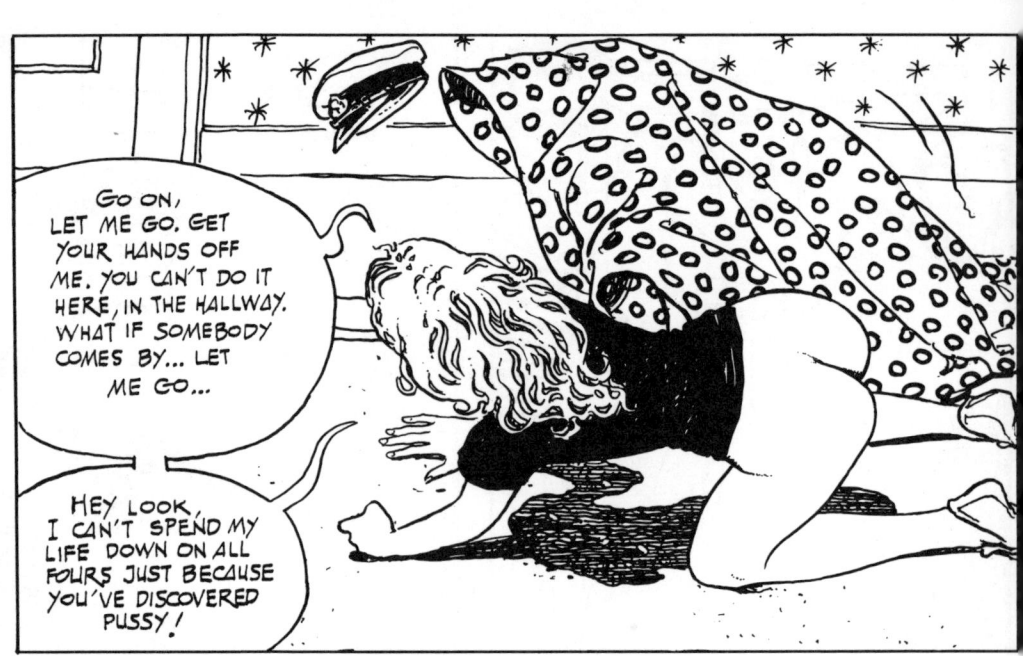

BEATRICE, TREASURE IT'LL BE STARTING IN TEN MINUTES!...

CAN YOU SMELL IT, TOO, THAT SICKENING BUTTERSCOTCH FLAVOR?

DON'T TALK LIKE AN ASSHOLE! ONLY HONEY WOULD USE SHIT LIKE THAT!

THE THEATER IS STANDING-ROOM-ONLY!

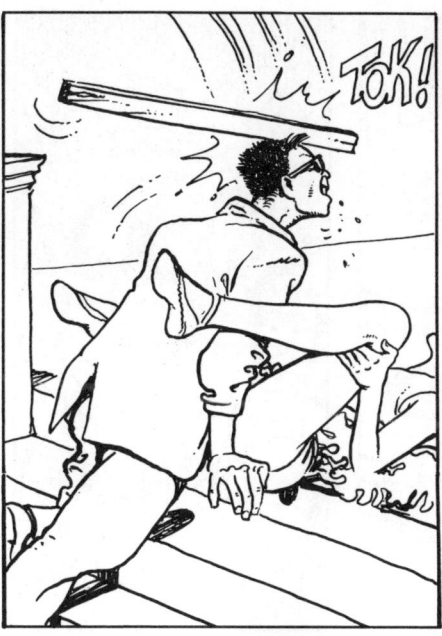

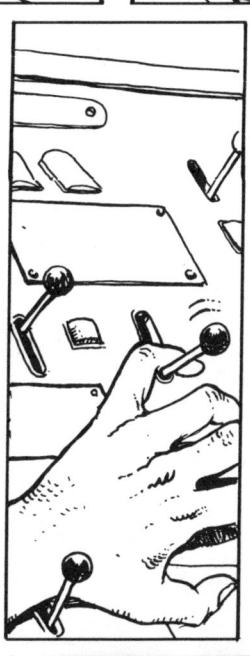

HEY! BOB! WHERE DID YOU GO?

THE CURTAIN IS UP! GO AHEAD WITH THE CAMERA! WE'RE ALREADY ON SATELLITE HOOK-UP!

OH! THERE YOU ARE! HHHMM!... I GOT IT... YOU WENT TO TAKE YOUR CLOTHES OFF, YOU NASTY LITTLE...

THE END